The Sidewal Rescue

by Hazel Hutchins
art by Ruth Ohi

ANNICK PRESS

TORONTO * NEW YORK * VANCOUVER

We acknowledge the support of the Canada Council for the Arts, the Ontario Arts Council, the Government of Ontario through the Ontario Book Publishers Tax Credit program and the Ontario Book Initiative, and the Government of Canada through the Book Publishing Industry Development Program (BPIDP) for our publishing activities.

Cataloging in Publication

Hutchins, H. J. (Hazel J.)
        The sidewalk rescue / by Hazel Hutchins ; art by Ruth Ohi.

ISBN 1-55037-831-7 (bound).--ISBN 1-55037-830-9 (pbk.)

        I. Ohi, Ruth II. Title.

PS8565.U826S53 2004   jC813'.54   C2003-904836-5

The art in this book was rendered in watercolor.
The text was typeset in Leawood Book.

Distributed in Canada by: Published in the U.S.A. by Annick Press (U.S.) Ltd.
Firefly Books Ltd.   Distributed in the U.S.A. by:
66 Leek Crescent   Firefly Books (U.S.) Inc.
Richmond Hill, ON   P.O. Box 1338
L4B 1H1   Ellicott Station
                                   Buffalo, NY 14205

Manufactured in China.

Visit us at: www.annickpress.com

For Sara and Annie
—H.H. and R.O.

The day Morgan's little sister drew a beautiful picture on the sidewalk and then jumped right inside to pick the flowers, Morgan raced into the house to tell her parents.

"Help, help, help!" she cried. "Josie is being chased by a huge, gigantic, mean and nasty lion."

It was true. A huge, gigantic, mean and nasty lion had leapt from the grasses and was chasing Josie toward the river.

"Do something!" cried Morgan.

Morgan's mother quickly took the box of chalk. She drew a boat at the riverbank and Josie scrambled aboard.

"That should do it," said Morgan's mother as Josie pushed off from the shore.

But Morgan did not think that would do it at all.

"Help, oh help!" she cried. "Josie is heading for a steep, deep, and ever so dangerous waterfall!"

Morgan's father quickly took the chalk box. He drew a pair of enormous talons wrapped very carefully around Josie's waist. Then he drew a great eagle attached to the talons.

"Up we go," smiled Morgan's father as the eagle lifted Josie away.

But Morgan was not smiling.

"The eagle is flying higher and higher and Josie is looking heavier and heavier!" cried Morgan.

It was true. The eagle was getting tired from carrying Josie. High over the mountains, it let go.

A lady walking by with her dog quickly picked up the chalk box.

"I can help," she said.

She drew a thick slope of fluffy snow.

"Thank you," said Morgan as Josie landed in the snow.

"I think …" added Morgan as Josie began to tumble.

"Look out!" cried Morgan. "Josie has turned into a giant snowball."

Snowball Josie was rolling over and over down the slope at tremendous speed straight toward a cliff.

A bicycle rider screeched to a stop. He took up the chalk box. He drew a ski jump to rescue Josie from the rocks below.

"Yahooo!" he cried as the snowball sailed safely upward off the ski jump.

But Morgan saw nothing to yahoo about.

"Help! Help! Help!" she cried. "The sun is melting Snowball Josie."

Josie was flying higher and higher into the air. The sun had already melted the snowball, and now it was beginning to melt Josie too.

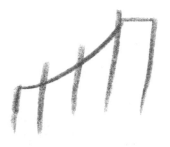

Ronnie, the neighbor across the street, came racing. He took the chalk and drew a cloud over the sun.

"That's got it," said Ronnie.

But Morgan did not think that got it at all.

"Josie is falling again!" she cried.

The mail carrier rushed over, threw down his mailbag, and picked up the chalk. He drew an entire ocean of water for Josie to land in.

Down among the beautiful corals and the fishes plunged Josie—but trouble was already headed her way.

"Sharrrrrrk!" cried Morgan.

"Sharrrrrrrrrrrrk!"

Even Josie couldn't swim faster than a shark.

An electrical worker slid down
a power pole. She took the chalk.
Just in time she drew an underwater
cave with an opening only large
enough for Josie.

"Quick, air!" said Morgan.
"Josie needs air. She
needs to be on the
surface again."

And the electrical worker added
a tunnel up to a sandy beach. "Now
Josie's safe," she nodded.

It was a lovely beach with palm
trees and friendly parrots for
company. For a moment, Morgan
thought everything was OK …

... and then she saw it—a great wall of water was moving toward the land.

"Tidal wave!"cried Morgan.

There was only one piece of chalk left.

"Sandbags!" cried Josie's mother.

"Wings!" cried Josie's father.

"Rescue helicopter!" cried the lady walking the dog.

"Life jacket!" cried the bicycler.

"Surfboard!" cried Ronnie.

"Whales to the rescue!" cried the mail carrier.

"Body armor!" cried the electrical worker.

But this time Morgan herself had taken up the last piece of chalk. Frantically she began drawing steps across the sand. Each step was a little bigger than the last. On and on along the sidewalk Morgan drew the steps, right up to their very own front door, where she drew the biggest step of all.

And the next
moment, there
was Josie with a
bouquet of flowers
in her hand.

"I picked these for you, Morgan, because you are the best sister in the world," said Josie.

Everyone heaved a great sigh of relief.

"Has anyone seen my dog?" asked the lady.

"Did you notice there is water in your basement?" asked Ronnie.

"I had a nightmare like this once," said the bicycler.

"My mailbag is full of sand and fish," said the mail carrier.

"I wonder if coconuts can be used on power poles," said the electrical worker.

But Morgan and Josie didn't notice.
Josie had taken a brand new box of
chalk from her pocket and was busy
drawing pictures of castles and knights
and dragons all along the sidewalk.